For Missy
who is
terrific
× × ×

Also by Sophy Henn

Where Bear?

Pom Pom Panda Gets the Grumps

Philomel Books

an imprint of Penguin Random House LLC

375 Hudson Street, New York, NY 10014

Library of Congress Cataloging-in-Publication Data is available upon request.

Manufactured in China by RR Donnelley Asia Printing Solutions Ltd. | ISBN 9780399547751

1 3 5 7 9 10 8 6 4 2

Text set in New Clarendon MT Std.

It On

by

Sophy Henn

When YOU see something TERRIFIC...

. . . smile a smile
and pass it on.

If you chance upon a chuckle,

hee hee hee
and pass it on.

If something happens
that's amazing,
whoop it up
and pass it on.

Should you spot
a thing of wonder,

jump for joy
and **pass it on.**

With all the smiles you have made
and the joy you've spread about,
you'll find the world's
a little nicer . . .

and those smiles
a little brighter.

Sometimes the fun and glee
        aren't in their usual place.
But search around,
        there's always some . . .

a hum, a hug, a happy face.

So when the sky
is gray and rainy,
you'll know just what to do . . .

grab your wellies and your coat,

splash a smile and pass it on.

If you feel a little lonely,
    don't let that worry you.
Just branch out,
    see who's there,

find some fun

and pass it on.

And when you least expect it,
like a bolt out of the blue,
a smile or a chuckle
will be passed . . .

right back to you.

Enjoy that happy moment,
let that feeling fill you up!

Then . . .

Have a ball,
   raise the roof,
kick your heels
      and . . .

pass
it
on!

Huge thanks to two things of wonder, Alice and Goldy